I0610735

The Long Way Around

Tooth and Nail

© Copyright 2021 by John Cash - All rights reserved.

The content contained within this book may not be reproduced, duplicated or transmitted without direct written permission from the author or the publisher.
Under no circumstances will any blame or legal responsibility be held against the publisher, or author, for any damages, reparation, or monetary loss due to the information contained within this book. Either directly or indirectly.

Legal Notice:
This book is copyright protected. This book is only for personal use. You cannot amend, distribute, sell, use, quote or paraphrase any part, or the content within this book, without the consent of the author or publisher.

Disclaimer Notice:
Please note the information contained within this document is for educational and entertainment purposes only. All effort has been executed to present accurate, up to date, and reliable, complete information. No warranties of any kind are declared or implied. Readers acknowledge that the author is not engaging in the rendering of legal, financial, medical or professional advice. The content within this book has been derived from various sources. Please consult a licensed professional before attempting any techniques outlined in this book.
By reading this document, the reader agrees that under no circumstances is the author responsible for any losses, direct or indirect, which are incurred as a result of the use of information contained within this document, including, but not limited to, — errors, omissions, or inaccuracies

Table of Contents

CHAPTER ONE

Friday, March 10 - Philadelphia

FBI Headquarters

"Okay, Hank. There's just something not quite lining up about this whole thing. Your explanation seems reasonable on the surface, but here's the thing: I received copies of the same receipts and a letter describing what they were, along with a photo of the packet that was sent to Daven. It exactly matches this one." He tapped the yellow envelope unnecessarily. "We launched an investigation immediately, and our conclusions are the exactly same as yours: the signatures cannot be confirmed either as genuine or fake, and the cashier checks are untraceable to a specific person without obtaining a warrant for the security footage from the location where they were purchased."

Hank swallowed his surprise in a too-large gulp of coffee, which burned his mouth painfully. His eyes watered, and he had to cough a few times before responding.

"You knew about this already? For how long?"

Stewart didn't answer that. "The Treasury Department traced all six purchases to a notorious bail bonds complex in San Bernardino. We've not had much luck with them before because their security cameras aren't the best quality, but we're working on it."

"Oh…"

"So my first question is, why didn't you inform us of this alleged plot the moment you discovered it?"

"I told you. I learned of it on March 4, when I was pretty much on my deathbed and out of the office. There was no point informing you when I didn't have enough information to hold a fruitful discussion. That was less than a week ago."

"You should have told me immediately, regardless. To do otherwise invited suspicion. I brought you here to see if you can help us launch a special investigation, which will allow us to obtain the warrant we need without pressing formal charges. But I can't do that at the moment."

"Why not?" Hank asked, feeling the world spin a little, in both directions somehow.

"Because there's a huge hole in your story that's yet to be explained. We know that Daven personally received the receipts at his house on February 13. So please don't tell me again that you weren't aware of them until March 4. On the surface, it looks like you held back investigating until after the March 1 vote in order to avoid negative publicity, which would have influenced your rallies."

"As I said, I only learned about them on March 4," Hank repeated hotly. "That is the truth. How do you know for sure that was the date he received them? Mail gets delayed all the time."

"I'm not at liberty to say how, but it's simply not up for debate," Stewart replied reluctantly. High-powered surveillance across the street had clearly captured Daven quizzically studying the bright yellow packet as he took his mail inside his house the evening of February 13, but the mere existence of that camera was strictly FBI knowledge.

"Not at liberty, huh? Well, I might not be 'at liberty' at all if this isn't figured out."

"That's what I'm here for. What happened to that packet between February 13 and March 4?"

Hank sat up straighter. "Was there anything illegal about us not informing you right away that we were investigating a possible forgery of an *internal* financial document? In fact, did we have any obligation at all to inform you of their existence until we had reached a conclusion of *our own* self-conducted investigation on *our own* employees, including myself?"

Stewart hesitated, then leaned back with a small sigh and shake of his head. "Technically, no."

Hank picked up his coffee again. "Exactly. Let's move on, then."

"I'm the one controlling this conversation, Hank, and we're staying on this topic for a minute. Since you claim you didn't know of their existence until March 4, I have to conclude that Daven himself - not you - held them back in order to wait for the March 1 vote to take place first. Possibly influenced and/or aided by Rupert. If that's the case, I need to know, because it will mitigate the circumstances and shift some of the blame away from you. Is that what happened?"

"Not even close."

"Then what? I need to give the president an explanation of some kind. Preferably one that's plausible, if you have one."

Hank leaned forward and set his cup down hard, causing a bit of coffee to splash onto the desk.

"I'd like to ask my question again, just for clarification. Was there anything illegal about our confidential investigation, or lack thereof? I seem to recall that you confirmed there wasn't, not even thirty seconds ago."

"Technically? No. But if it was delayed specifically to influence the vote? Absolutely. Looking at a felony on that one."

"Well, good luck trying to prove it."

Stewart stood up and shoved his chair back into the credenza in frustration. "I've had enough of this, Hank. I'm trying to help you, and you're stonewalling me at every opportunity. Go back to Los Angeles, and report here again on Monday afternoon if you've come to your senses by then. If not, I'll bring in Daven and Rupert instead to tell me *their* side of the story."

"They're busy on Monday. Monthly birthday luncheon at the office. How's Tuesday looking for you?"

Stewart raised an eyebrow at him. "You're being awfully cocky and defensive today. More so than usual. Are you sure that's in your best interests?"

"Are you sure that continuing this conversation is in my best interests?"

"Yes, because you're bluffing. I know you. You would never agree to let me summon Rupert and Daven here."

"Do it," muttered Hank as he reached over to pluck a Kleenex out of the holder and wiped up the spilled coffee to buy a few seconds to think. His bravado was failing as he realized the line was behind him now; he had crossed it with that simple *do it.*

Stewart sat back down and watched him for a few moments. Quietly he said, "Hank. I like you. I trust you. And you *know* that has always been true, despite our conflicts. Why don't you just tell me what's really going on in your head right now? If you don't, I'm going to have to transfer this case to someone else, because it appears my days of getting through to you are over. That's not a threat. If I fail to do my job and get enough information from you, an entire month of my time will have been wasted on trying to figure out how to exonerate you. I think I can guarantee that the next person who steps into this mess won't be nearly as enthusiastic."

Oh shit, thought Hank.

Stewart continued, "I'm not judging you for being defensive and angry. I'm not concluding you did anything wrong, or right, or whatever. But your behavior towards me - the *only* person in the position to help you right now - is indefensible, and I won't put up with it for one more minute. Tell me how you want to proceed. It's your choice."

Silence.

Stewart flopped his notebook shut after a minute of waiting in vain for Hank to speak again. "Alright. I'll summon Rupert and Daven, then. You can go."

"No. Leave them out of it," Hank said finally, giving up the bluff. "Daven held on to the receipts because he was afraid to confront me. Avoiding bad PR never even occurred to him, because his mind doesn't work that way. If they had gone to Rupert first, it's possible *he* would have held them back for that reason. Likely, even. But not Dav, and I would gladly bet my own life and career on that."

"What changed his mind about telling you?"

"Don't know. I never asked."

"It's good he revealed them when he did. We were waiting to see what you would do, and I was getting nervous. If he had destroyed them, or hid them from-"

"He would've *never* done that!" Hank retorted fiercely. "Even to imply it, or think that for one second, is, is-"

"I believe you. Calm down."

Stewart opened his notebook back up again and wrote for some time, then closed it one last time.

"Thank you for your honesty, however belated. Even if you aren't convicted of bribery, it's possible Daven could be publicly censured."

Hank's temper flared to new heights. "There is nothing illegal about what he did. You said so yourself!"

"A broken law isn't a requirement for censure. Poor judgment is usually enough, and I can hardly think of a more worthy example than that. At any rate, at least this makes me feel comfortable to launch a special investigation and get that warrant, which I'll proceed with on Monday."

"Okay. Well...thank you?"

"Don't thank me. I hate this as much as you do."

He looked over Hank's shoulder as his secretary caught his attention through the glass.

"Come in."

"Sorry to interrupt. The president is asking to see both of you in five minutes."

"Thank you."

The door closed, and Hank raised his eyebrows. "May I ask what *this* is going to be about?"

"Yes, we should have discussed it already but this thing with the receipts has taken all our time. Prepare yourself, Hank. It's highly likely that President Rickon is going to invalidate the passing of your upcoming measure."

"What! Why?"

"Walk with me, it's going to take a minute to get to the conference room." As they were hurrying down a long, empty hall, Stewart said in a low voice, "The rumor about you offering to bribe Gamble is running rampant, and he wants to talk about formally investigating in order to avoid accusations and bad PR. It's inevitable that the charges will be dropped due to lack of recordings, but the measure will get put back at the end of the line to go through the house again...probably to be put on the July or August voting docket."

Hank's anger resurfaced instantly, and he stopped in his tracks. "Are you serious? Not acceptable. There is zero evidence. I refuse to meet with him until these '*charges*' are dropped."

Stewart gaped at him. "But you haven't even been charged yet, and you might not be if the president approves to drop it. That's what this conversation is about, and you're lucky to get an audience with him at all."

"No. I won't be any part of it. Let me know when you're all done jerking me around."

"You can't just refuse to talk to the president. Come on."

"Oh, really? Let me show you how it's done."

Hank turned on his heel and made a beeline towards the back exit that led to his waiting car.

Stewart quickly caught up to him. "Stop being an idiot, Hank. Seriously, this is a huge mistake."

Hank kept walking, and Stewart followed in silence for the two minutes it took to traverse the hallway. When they reached the little lobby, Stewart snapped his fingers at the security desk, and the exit instantly locked itself with a resonating *clang*. Hank tried pushing it anyway, in vain, then stood there and just shook his head.

"You can't be serious," he grumbled under his breath as two guards came up to the men and kept a respectful but cautious distance.

Stewart was completely done with Hank's attitude, but he forced his tone to stay calm and gentle. "You can either come with me to talk to the president now, or we can formally indict you on bribery charges and have you held in Philadelphia until the investigation is completed. Your choice."

Hank laughed humorlessly. "Oh, I see. So I guess this means you're no longer on my side?" he challenged.

"Stop being so dramatic. If I *wasn't* on your side, I would just let you leave."

Hank looked out at his waiting car and did a double take. Avery had pulled up too hastily upon sight of him and accidentally jumped a good portion of the sidewalk with both right tires. Hank made a mental note to tease him for it later. Right now, there was nothing more he wanted than to dive in the backseat and speed off to the airport, back to the relative safety of his new house. But...*fuck it all.*

"Unlock the door," said Hank wearily.

Stewart turned to the security desk and nodded, and the door unhitched itself with a mechanical asshole. Hank strode up to the car and leaned into the open window.

"Don't quit your day job to become a valet."

"Sorry, boss. These streets are crazy narrow."

"Yeah. I just got called into another meeting. Need you to go back and wait a little longer, unfortunately."

"Will do."

"Thanks. See you in a bit. Stay off the sidewalk."

He went back in, turned to Stewart and began walking again, his former good humor partially restoring itself along the way.

"Nice trick," he remarked coolly. "I deserved that. Sorry for being a dick."

"Well, desperate times and all that. I'm sorry for threatening you. You know I don't want any of this to go south, so..."

Hank cleared his throat. "Yeah. Thanks. It's too bad you're my FBI handler. I think we could have been good friends in another life. You remind me so much of Daven sometimes."

Stewart laughed. "Having met Daven on one of his more awkward days, I'm not sure that's much of a compliment. But thank you."

"It's the highest compliment, I assure you. He does infuriate me to the core sometimes, but you can probably guess who's fault that is. Anyway, what would you suggest I say to president Rickon regarding this whole thing?"

"Nothing much. Just listen, agree to do what he says, and scoot the hell out while you have the chance. He's been in a mood lately. At least take solace in the fact that you're not the only person he's pissed off at today."

"Oh. Good. I think."

CHAPTER TWO

FBI Headquarters, Philadelphia

Friday, March 10

Hank wasn't allowed into the conference room upon arrival; the president wanted to speak with Stewart first. Hank was obligated to wait a respectful distance away, and was not permitted to take out his phone. That gave him plenty of time to observe Rickon's dozen-strong security detail, which was remarkable for the fact that nearly all of them were female.

Hank suddenly regretted having all male servants and guards for so long, because Brittany had been an outstanding (and overdue) addition to the household, with unique strengths that the men never had developed. Like a maternal instinct, for example. That's why she was usually assigned to guard his sons. For the first time, he wondered what it must be like for her to live amongst 17 men and two boys...even the dogs were male. Most of the guards only lived at the house four days a week (the servants were 5 days), but Brittany was one of three who lived there full-time (along with Avery and Vance). He made a mental note to check and make sure all of her needs were being taken care of, as far as her accommodations and-

Hank dismissed this train of thought abruptly as Salome Danby suddenly strode into the anteroom carrying a binder

that was much too small for the amount of contents it contained. Hank recognized it instantly as being Stewart's file on him; Salome must have stopped into his office to grab it in the way here. She darted into the conference room without a glance at anyone, and all was quiet again.

So quiet that Hank imagined he could hear his heart pounding and blood rushing. Or maybe he *wasn't* imagining it.

————

Seditionists Headquarters

Daven's Office

"What do you think is happening now?" Rupert asked for a second time as he sat across the table from Daven, who was busy being ridiculously picky about editing the long-delayed media statement to address the March 1 vote.

"I don't know. How could I *possibly* know?"

"I'm just trying to make conversation."

"And I'm just trying to work," Dav replied, a telling edge to his tone that indicated he was under more stress than usual. "Which is exactly what you should be doing, too. How's it coming with that list?"

"It's coming." Rupert sighed as he looked at his written notes. Hank requested a comprehensive list of all the headlines pertaining to him that he had missed during his illness, and Rupert had to write them out by hand because he had spilled orange juice all over his laptop yesterday and was still waiting for a replacement. He threw the pen down and massaged the painful muscle between his thumb and index finger. *Feels like I'm in school again* , he grumbled to himself.

"Sorry, what was that?" Daven asked without taking his eyes off his own task.

"Nothing."

"Let me see the list."

Rupert took a deep breath and gave him the notebook, swallowing his resentment for the hundredth time in ten days. He really didn't like Daven lording it over him like this. As usual, not having Hank around for so long drastically altered the dynamics between the longtime friends, to the point where Rupe always felt like nothing he did would be ever good enough for Daven. Like a little kid constantly trying to please his father. *Like Floyd* .

Daven put the list down, frowning. "This is taking too long. He wants it done before he leaves Philadelphia, so he can review it on the plane."

"I know, Dav. You do recall that he only asked me two days ago, right? I still have dozens of papers to go through, and then I have to type up this damned thing."

Daven grunted. "I'll start typing it up to save time. You keep reviewing the papers. Three hours. Not a minute longer."

"I *know,* for fuck's sake!"

That got Daven to finally look up, but he said nothing. He didn't have to; they both knew from past experience that Hank would nail Rupe to the wall if he disrespected Dav's authority in his absence. Like he was doing now.

"Right," Rupe said as cheerfully as he could manage. "Three hours. Got it."

Daven nodded as he moved over to his computer, taking Rupe's notebook with him.

"Dav?" said Rupe quietly a moment later as he hovered at the door. "I'm really worried about Hank. That's all. Sorry I've been a pain."

Daven picked up his fourth cup of espresso and peered over the monitor. "Hank can handle himself. Can you?"

———————

FBI HQ - Philadelphia

Hank Bancroft was not handling himself well. The president was in a snippy, take-no-prisoners mood, and Hank was all but rising to every provocation that had come up since he walked in the door after waiting almost two hours like a schoolboy waiting to see the principal.

First to irritate him was the insistence from the president on addressing him as *Mr. Bancroft* . He was no longer simply Hank, because he was in trouble and it had to be keep being emphasized for some reason, in case he missed it. He did not; Rickon made his feelings on the matters quite clear.

Apparently Stewart and Salome had just laid everything out on the table that was going on with Hank and the Seditionists, and now it was time for the reckoning.

So that meant that secondly, Hank was entirely unappreciative of being ambushed by three people at once, and he made his feelings known. So did the president, who had similar feelings.

"You want to talk about being ambushed? How about me having to sit here today listening to 90 minutes' worth of bullshit going in your party. Rather, in one of this *nation's* political parties. You think it's all about you!"

"Which particular instance of bullshit are you referring to?" Hank fired back.

"You haven't talked to Harmon in several weeks, against our express instructions, is that correct?"

"Yes. He tried to-"

"Don't care," snapped the president. "Get it together, you're not children. And what's this about Daven holding back knowledge of a bribery scheme-"

Hank bristled. " *Forgery* scheme."

"Alleged forgery scheme, then, which conveniently he only informed you about after the March 1 vote? I have a mind to completely invalidate that day's measures, but I won't go that far since I think they're for the good of the nation."

"I see. Glad you agree that flaying the skin off human beings in front of children and women is probably a bad thing."

"Among other things, including your attitude. You're on dangerous ground, Mr. Bancroft. I expect you to address me respectfully from this point on."

Stewart and Salome were frozen in place, faces white. Apparently they did not see the president in this mood very often, and it was for damned certain they never saw anyone talk to him like that before. Hank picked up his water bottle and took an enormous gulp, then capped it again and set it down hard.

"With all due *respect* I find it interesting, sir, that you added the word *alleged* before the words *forgery scheme* , but you did not add it before *bribery scheme* . Do we not practice 'innocent until proven guilty' in this country anymore? You're the president, you know best, and I would be grateful if you could condescend to educate me on that point."

Hank got kicked out of the conference room for that comeback - discussion over - and was now sitting alone in Stewart's office again. He was running an hour late to catch his plane, and thought of poor Avery, who must be bored to tears waiting for him in the lobby with absolutely nothing to do.

When Stewart returned, Hank was shocked to see him in a state of open amusement.

"Holy shit, Hank. How the hell do you walk around with balls that big? I'm truly intrigued….please condescend to educate me on that point."

"Anti-chafing powder is a must. Buy it in bulk."

"Noted."

Despite his joking, Hank was more anxious than he had ever been in his life, save for Floyd and Theo going missing once for two hours. He knew he had gone too far with Rickon once again, and had been busy imagining all sorts of dire consequences in his head while waiting for Stewart to return.

"So? Am I fired, arrested, or what? Don't keep me in suspense."

Stewart smiled a little. "None of the above. You made your point, and the president has agreed to drop the matter regarding Colton Gamble."

"Oh." Shit, that was unexpected. "But not the receipts, I take it?"

Now Stewart was serious again. "No. In fact..." He opened his binder and pulled out six printed sheets. "Sorry to inform you that you're now under official investigation for that. We need your statement on all of these outstanding items in my file. A number of questionable items are being examined, some of which-"

"This is ridiculous," Hank said tightly.

"Let me finish. Your written explanation, in as many words as necessary, due in 14 days. In person. The president feels this is more... *suited to your temperament* , he said, to give you the opportunity to offer your thoughts in writing."

"What?" Hank numbly reached out for the papers, but Stewart didn't hand them over.

"No, I need to rephrase and clarify some of these items. Maybe add a few. They'll go out Fed-Ex tomorrow, to reach you Monday."

"What kind of questions?"

Stewart looked at the first paper. "One of them is in regards to Daven's motivations for holding back the receipts."

"I already told you."

"The second one...and these are not in chronological order, by the way...is in regards to calls you made to an unlisted

Colorado mobile number on December. Things like that. Some of these are probably trivial."

Hank felt like he was going to have a heart attack. "Trivial? To whom?"

Stewart sat back in his chair, looking regretful. "Sorry. That was the wrong word. What I meant is that some of them are completely unrelated to the *alleged* forgery scheme . The president wants a full picture of all your activities since right before Janet's murder. You can't deny that a lot of shit has been going down since then. Mystery calls, blackmail attempts, etc. It's all very suspicious to him. Not to me, so much. Political shenanigans like this have been going on since the rise of mankind. But he's the boss, and we have to answer these questions for him."

Hank set his jaw and did not waver. "I told you. I'm being framed."

"And I heard you, but Hank...you have to prove it to me. Or at least give me something to go on. Someone to point the finger at. This is your chance. I'm working on it too, you know. Still trying to track down these cashier's checks to see who bought them. That could crack open everything. Trying to save you is becoming my full time job."

Hank's blood froze. *Trying to save you. Which means...I need saving. Which means...I'm in danger. From what?*

Stewart sighed and closed his binder and put the papers away. "There's one last thing. Your daily calls with Harmon must resume on Monday. Absolutely no excuses. If you fail to comply, you'll get your third warning. The final warning is after that, and you know what that means."

When Hank was able to speak again, it sounded to his own ears that his voice was 100 feet away from his mouth. "What you said earlier...that you're trying to 'save me.' Did you mean that literally?"

Stewart cleared his throat. "Literally? What do you mean?"

Hank knew then. Stewart was holding back. It was there in his eyes, clear as day. They had something else on him. Something darker than he could presently imagine. There was no doubt. That explained the wiretapping, among other things. *What the fuck...*

"Hank? You okay?"

"Quick question. Were you guys wiretapping my old house?"

Stewart looked startled for half a second, but then his guard instantly went up again. "You know I can't answer that."

"You were. I *know* you were. I heard it. That's why I disconnected the lines. Why did you do it?"

"Hank."

Hank felt horribly sick and dizzy all of a sudden, like the flu was starting all over again. But maybe this was the tail end of it; after all, he still had a slight fever only yesterday.

"I need to go home. Haven't seen my boys in ten days."

"Okay, we're done now. I'll see you on March...seriously, are you alright? You're white as a sheet." He reached into his refrigerator and grabbed another bottle of water. By the time he turned back around, Hank was passed out on the floor.

When Hank came to, he was surrounded by Avery and two female medics. Stewart was nowhere in sight.

"Sorry," Hank said thickly. His pulse was rushing in his ears, and his tongue felt three times as big in his mouth. It was a disgustingly sickening sensation. "Overtaxed...been sick. I'm alright."

"If you can sit up, sir, try it very slowly," said one of the medics.

"Yeah, I'm good. I got this."

Hank sat up and was treated to the sight of the office spinning in circles around him. The medics took his medical history and some vitals, and some kind of heart test, and determined he was going to be fine. Hank quickly recovered and Stewart reluctantly gave up his attempt to get an ambulance to transport him to the hospital. Hank was over two hours late for his flight home. The boys would be very annoyed by the delay, that was for sure. Probably Daven, too. He had to be sick of their bickering after ten days.

Seditionist HQ - Los Angeles - 2pm

Daven was grateful for the delay in Hank's return, because three hours had not been enough to complete the task. But five hours had. Rupert walked into his office to hand the rest of the list over, and then thanked his friend for typing everything out.

"No problem. Let me send this to Hank while you're here. Don't go. Close the door, please."

Within five minutes Dav had typed out the rest of the list (Rupert was always in awe of how fast his typing was; the fingers were nearly a blur) and emailed it to Hank. Then he closed his laptop with a decisive snap and looked over to where Rupert was sitting stiffly on the couch.

"I got a call from Hank," he said. "He's in the air by now. Will be home before 9.

"Did he say how the meeting went?"

"No, nothing. Which means-"

"-he got a serious beat down from Stewart," Rupert finished for him. "Or Salome."

"Or the president."

"Or all three of them."

Daven then did something incredibly out of character, and nearly unbelievable. Something that left Rupert's jaw metaphorically on the floor for a good amount of time.

Dav decided to leave the office early. It almost defied reality.

"Wait, what? Dav? Is that you? I'm hearing things. I'm in the Twilight Zone. Who *are* you?"

Daven went to his closet and took his coat off the hanger. "I'm someone badly in need of a break. And so are you. You're leaving, too."

Rupert stared at him. "I can't. I have a thousand things to do. At least."

"Not anymore. I'm the boss for three more hours, and I say we're done for the day. Let's go."

So they went. Daven chose Rupe's favorite bar at the end of Santa Monica pier, where they drank themselves silly and ate junk food until home school ended. Then they staggered back to their respective homes, accompanied by their bemused guards, to sort out the kids and return to real life.

Santa Monica Airport - 7:30pm

"Hey, Dav. I'm so sorry I'm late. Just touched down. I'll be there by eight."

"No problem. The boys are eagerly waiting for you."

"My house, or yours?"

"Yours."

"Okay, thanks. You okay?" Hank asked in concern. "You sound a little...were you asleep?"

"Yes, I am," Daven admitted. "I was, rather. Went to happy hour with Rupert. Knocked me out."

Hank felt himself grinning. He liked it when Daven loosened up, which was an increasingly rare occurrence. "That's great, Dav. Good. Glad you made time to go have some fun."

"I have a confession, Hank. Our particular happy hour commenced at 2:30pm."

"Oh, shit. Drinking on the job, huh? That's new."

"We went to the pier. I'm sorry. It was irresponsible and I take full blame for it."

Again, Hank grinned. "You don't always have to tell me *everything* , Dav. I wouldn't have asked. As long as you had a good time. I know it's been a difficult week. I'm only mad that I wasn't there to enjoy it with you. Anyway, thanks for the list of headlines. It wasn't as bad as I feared, especially the more recent ones. Looks like people are starting to calm the fuck down about the flogging initiative and focusing on other things. Like how much I'm leaving you in my will after I die of the plague."

Daven found himself shuddering at the thought. "Did you see the one that diagnosed you with bi-polar disorder? Or yellow fever?"

"Yeah. Surprised there aren't rumors out there that I'm pregnant. Goddamned paparazzi. Anyway, thanks again."

"Please thank Rupert, not me. He did all of the work on that, and my only contribution was to email it to you."

"I will. Thanks. See you in a bit."

"See you soon."

Daven set down the phone, and then turned around to find Floyd watching him with a wide smile. "Ha, I knew it! You were way too happy when you got home to be sober. Theo owes me ten bucks."

CHAPTER THREE

Bancroft House

Same evening

Hank exhausted himself into apathy on the flight home with all the thinking and worrying. By the time they were over Utah, he didn't care about his career, didn't care about the Seditionists, didn't care about the president. Nothing mattered for the time being, and it was refreshing to just focus on getting in bed and sleeping through the weekend. He was even seriously thinking of bailing on church for the second Sunday in a row, even though it would give the media (and his executives) a collective stroke.

The boys greeted him somberly at the front door, and Hank instantly picked up on their complete lack of enthusiasm at the sight of him. It hurt a little. A lot, if he was going to be totally honest with himself. He always suspected they liked their Uncle Dav better than him.

"Oh my god, dad," blurted Theo fearfully as he backed away. "You look so skinny."

Daven's eyes were almost as wide as Theo's. "Good to see you, Hank."

"Good to be back. Bit of a day."

"Did you bring us any pretzels, dad?" Floyd asked brightly - perhaps a little *too* brightly - after an awkward silence from the group.

"Of course. Have I ever come back empty-handed from Philly? In my grey bag. We kept them in the warmer on the plane this time, so they should still be fresh. I brought you some other goodies, too. Go look."

The boys lit up and finally stepped forward to greet him with silent hugs that lacked power - as if they were afraid to break him - but it was better than nothing. When they darted off to scramble through Hank's luggage he took the opportunity to go in the kitchen and grab a root beer for himself, and a ginger ale for Dav.

"Do you have a minute to talk?" Daven asked gingerly, quietly.

"About a minute is all I have left in me. My study."

--

Hank shut the door, then flopped down on his couch and stretched. "Do I really look *that* bad?"

"Yes, you do. What happened today?"

He wasn't about to tell Dav he had face-planted in Stewart's office, so he kept his tone light. "I got myself into a bit of trouble again, but I don't want to talk about it until Monday. It can keep. How were the boys? Did they act up? God, I was so sick. Thank you for taking such great care of them. I don't even think I even asked you once how they were doing."

"No, you didn't, because you know I would have told you if anything was wrong. We had some minor problems, but they were instructed to tell you personally. I'd rather not roll them under the bus."

"*Throw* , Dav. Not roll. It's better if you tell me, so I can hear it from multiple points of view."

Daven leaned against the desk. He couldn't take his eyes off Hank. He looked like a different person. Leaner, darker, wearier. Dangerous. It was frightening.

"How much weight did you lose?" he asked worriedly.

"Dav . Don't change the subject. I want to know if the boys behaved. If you don't prepare me, Floyd is going to take the blame for everything Theo did, and Theo will let him. If you want to be their guardian, this is the kind of shit you have to deal with. What if something happens to me tomorrow and they get turned over to you-"

"Nothing's going to happen to you," Daven interrupted hastily, a little too urgently. Hank was a little startled by the harshness and immediacy of his tone, and the two men stared at each other for a long moment.

If only you knew that for sure. Because I don't.

Daven cleared his throat. "Alright, fine. A few days ago they were arguing over the bathroom, and Floyd shoved Theo to the floor. There were three times Theo talked back to Brittany, and the third time I had to step in and send him to his room. He apologized to her and didn't do it again. That was all. They're good kids, Hank, and smart. Rupert says they've never once misbehaved in home school, and all their work is done in time and thoroughly. So...maybe go easy on them?"

Too late. Hank's anger had already flared at the imagery of Floyd manhandling his little brother, and he had no intention of going easy on him for it. But he stayed calm and collected so that Dav wouldn't feel guilty for spilling the beans.

"Thanks for the recap. Listen...I've been thinking. Are you prepared to take care of these kids if something does happen to me? And don't say it won't, because we don't know. You're their legal guardian upon my death, but I can transfer that power to Rupert, if you have any hesitation whatsoever after having just spent ten days with them. And I know there's more you aren't telling me, but that's fine. As long as it was nothing major."

Daven looked alarmed for a flash of a second, then breathed deep and cocked his head. "What happened in Philadelphia?" he asked gently.

Hank ignored the question. "So let me know how you feel. I want to be sure all my paperwork is in order before my next trip. Okay?"

"When's your next trip?"

"Two weeks."

Daven didn't blink. "I have to be honest, Hank. The fact that you're asking me this right now, just after your return from 'getting in trouble in Philadelphia' is really scaring the hell out of me."

"No need, it's unrelated. We just had a really rough flight home, and I was thinking about morbid things like planes crashing and having a stroke from the stress of dealing with all this bullshit. I mean, you read those headlines. It's a miracle I haven't jumped off a bridge already. Look, Dav, I promise to tell you about Philadelphia on Monday. Every bit of it, in excruciating detail, okay? I'm too tired right now. Thanks so much for everything."

"Alright. I should get going, then. Goodnight."

Daven encountered Avery in the driveway as he walked back to his waiting car. They solemnly shook hands, and Daven decided to test out a theory. Something his instinct had just triggered.

"How was your flight? Looked like it might be rough, with all the storms everywhere."

"Smooth sailing. Hardly a bump, fortunately. You know how much I hate flying."

Rough flight, eh? God damn it, Hank... "I'm glad to hear it. See you Sunday morning."

Dav could hardly sleep that night. It was the first time in memory that he had caught Hank in an outright lie, and the realization stunned and frightened him. He wasn't ready to be a father to Floyd and Theo, and he would never be ready to accept that Hank wasn't going to be around forever. But something about Hank's manner told him he might have to start preparing to face both possibilities.

Saturday morning

Bancroft House

Floyd had made the most luxurious breakfast Hank had ever seen outside a fancy hotel, and it almost seemed a waste that only the three of them would be able to enjoy it. But alas, Avery was asleep, Brittany was at the dentist, and Vance was just too weird for table conversation. The other guards were all either on duty or about to head to the gun range.

"Boys," he said between bites of omelet, "I understand from Dav that there were a few disciplinary problems this past week. I trust that you will learn from whatever happened and not repeat it again. Is there anything major I should know about?"

Theo and Floyd lowered their forks and stared at their dad. Floyd spoke up once he had swallowed his huge mouthful of eggs. "Uncle Dav didn't tell you what I did?"

"Why don't *you* tell me?"

Floyd swallowed hard. "Theo and I were fighting over the bathroom, and I shoved him to the ground to get in first."

"That's not what happened!" Theo put in. "Dav came to yell at us-"

"Yell?" interrupted Hank, shocked.

Floyd set his fork down and got all dramatic, as he was prone to do when retelling a story. "He didn't yell! He was literally like (Floyd pitched his voice down as low as it could go) *hey hey kiddos, what's the solution to this problem* and we agreed to stop arguing. Don't exaggerate, Theo."

"You're exaggerating, not me," refuted Theo. "There was no fighting, dad. Floyd just likes to get us in trouble."

"No, I don't," Floyd replied in confusion.

"If you didn't you wouldn't have told him-"

Hank knocked on the table. "*Boys*. Enough. I'm sorry I asked. Floyd, we'll chat later."

Floyd nodded and squirmed in his chair. "It wasn't-"

"I said later."

Floyd wrung his hands together a little in his anxiety. "Okay, sorry."

"Mr. Bancroft?" called Lucas quietly from the living room. "Mr. Johansson is here to see you."

"Tell him to come join us for breakfast. Got quite a setup here."

Daven came in and talked to Lucas for a minute before joining the family. "I didn't mean to barge in on breakfast. I actually came to see if I could go the shooting range with your guards."

The boys instantly perked up at that, and looked at each other with shining eyes. Daven's talent on the range was legendary, and the boys were eager to see him in action after so many years of hearing about it. It was part of the reason they were so intimidated by him, because his outward personality offered no hint as to the lethal shooting machine that lay inside. Even Hank's well-honed accuracy couldn't hold a candle to Daven's incredible eye.

"Of course you can go," Hank answered. "You know you're always welcome. Want to eat first?"

Daven hesitated, looking uncomfortable. "Can I talk to you for a moment, please? In private."

Hank hated leaving his omelet to get cold, but Dav would obviously not bother him unless absolutely necessary, which meant something was wrong. His skin prickled uncomfortably as he followed Dav to the study.

"What's up?"

Daven pulled the Saturday morning newspaper out of his pocket, and Hank took it wordlessly. The first page of the Politics section headline read:

Urbanes Hacked, Seditionists Blamed

"What the fuck is this?" Hank exclaimed, even as he started reading the story. Written by Hailey, of course. Who else?

Daven sounded exhausted. "Long story short, Hank…Harmon's executive team had all of their personal information released in some kind of information dump that was sent out on a listserv last night. Phone numbers, addresses, payroll, financials, bank account numbers. Everything. All twenty of them. It's been sent everywhere, no taking it back."

Hank kept reading, and his heart stopped on this part: *…an anonymous insider claims this is a retaliatory measure perpetrated by Hank Bancroft, controversial leader of the Seditionists, who is no longer on speaking terms with Harmon for unknown reasons. As Mr. Bancroft was in Philadelphia on Friday and departed hours later than scheduled, it is assumed he or someone in his party has been placed under investigation for this latest political calamity.*

He is well known to employ double agents within the organization, and this is not the first time confidential information has been released to unauthorized parties. In October-

"Dav," Hank said shakily as he folded the paper back up. "This is exactly why I was asking you about guardianship of the boys."

Daven looked astonished. "You *knew* about this?"

"No, but I knew something big was coming. Something like this. Stewart...the way he was acting. *Fuck*. We need to talk. Now. Not here."

Hank quickly packed up his briefcase and went back out to the dining room.

"Lucas. Boys."

"Yaeghda?" Theo answered with a mouthful of chocolate milk.

"Go easy on that milk, Theo, it's a lot of sugar. Change of plans. I have to go to the office for a few hours, so the guards will take you to the range with them. Sit in the waiting room while they shoot, and do *not* bother them or ask to touch any guns. I swear to god if either of you misbehave, I'm taking my belt to you *both* when I get back, no questions asked. Understood?"

The boys nodded, faces white, and Hank left with Daven after throwing on a heavy coat.

Floyd watched the huge SUV pulling out of the driveway, which was immediately and closely tailed by all the press cars that had been rapidly accumulating within the past hour. Then he began having another panic attack.

CHAPTER FOUR

Seditionist HQ

Saturday, March 11

After two hours at the office talking in circles with Daven and Rupert and getting absolutely nowhere, Hank made an executive decision that the other two men strongly opposed: he called his rival.

"What the hell do you want?" Harmon answered irritably; he had not recognized the number and would never have picked up otherwise.

"Just wanted to tell you I have absolutely nothing to do with this so-called 'data dump.' Nothing. You *know* I would not lie to you."

"Don't ever call me again outside of the 10 minutes each weekday that I'm legally obligated to hear you breathe."

"I need your help trying to figure out-"

"Piss off." Hank stared at his phone as it disconnected, and then shrugged and dialed again. This time it went straight to voicemail.

"Don't leave a message, Hank," warned Daven. So Hank left a message, of course.

"Harmon, Hank here. This is my new cell number. Call me back today. We need to talk about this insider of yours who is accusing me of something he or she has absolutely no evidence for. I'll be pressing slander charges tomorrow, and need to know who to name in the lawsuit. If you don't tell me today who talked to Hailey, I'll name you, since what your employees say to reporters is ultimately your responsibility. Thank you."

"What the fuck, Hank?" Rupert asked in shock after Hank hung up. "Are you *insane?*"

Hank froze and stared at him with a ferocity that made Rupe want to be swallowed up by a hole in the floor.

"Excuse me?" Hank shot back icily. "So that's how you talk to your boss now?"

"Apparently I have to, because you're losing your goddamn mind!"

Hank bristled, so Daven stepped in between the two of them, his hands held up in a "calm down" gesture.

"Gentlemen, let's take a break."

"Go home, Rupert," said Hank irritably, peering over Daven's shoulder at him. "I don't need you right now if you're going to-"

"You don't need me at all anymore, looks like."

Daven rounded on Rupert. " *Stop it* . No one's going anywhere. Sit down, both of you, and start writing out the media statement before you have a stroke. I'll make us some more coffee."

————

Bancroft Home

"Just keep breathing slowly, Floyd. It's okay," coached Brittany, who had just returned from her dentist appointment in time to see the poor kid laid out on the couch for the third time this morning.

Avery had been awakened by the commotion and was now sitting anxiously nearby with Floyd's paper bag in one hand and a bottle of water in the other. "I'm going to call your dad."

"No," protested Floyd as he struggled to sit up. "I'm fine."

"Sorry, buddy, I have to. He's going to kill us already for waiting this long." He glared at Lucas, knowing he was in for a seriously bad time trying to explain this to Hank.

Floyd protested feebly, then threw up twice. Avery pulled out his phone while Brittany ran to get cleaning supplies.

- - - - - - -

Seditionist HQ

Hank Bancroft, leader of The Seditionists, has launched an internal investigation to determine whether anyone affiliated with his organization is responsible for the confidential data that was released-

"No," Hank said irritably, crossing out *anyone affiliated* and *responsible* on Rupert's third draft . "Try again."

Daven then out read his own edits to the draft: *Hank Bancroft, leader of The Seditionists, will immediately launch an internal investigation into the allegations.*

Hank looked up at his Chief of Staff. "Where's the rest? Or is that it?"

"That's it."

"Okay, um. No. Try again. Rupe?"

"Alright, how's this? *Hank Bancroft, leader of the The Seditionists, vehemently denies the allegations regarding his involvement and will immediately launch an internal investigation to determine whether any entity of his organization was involved in the incident.*"

"That's good. A bit cold, though. Warm it up a little, but keep the same words. My phone's ringing, hang on. Hey Avery."

"Sir, we need to take Floyd to the hospital. He just threw up some blood, not a lot."

"Shit. Like, out of the blue? Or has he been panicking?"

Avery took a deep breath, preparing himself for the rebuke of a lifetime. "He's been panicking. Hyperventilated three times since you left, I'm told."

"You were *told*?"

"Yes, sir, just woke up and came out to the living room to find him having his third attack. Still is."

"Alright. Whoever decided not to call me after the second one is fired. You can fill me in later. Take Floyd to Palisades, discreetly. I'll join you when I can."

"*When you can?*" Avery blurted, unable to stop himself from keeping the disgust out of his voice.

"You heard me correctly." Hank hung up, then turned back to the statement. "Dav, try changing it to *shocking and unacceptable incident.*"

Philadelphia

"Hi, it's Stewart. I just received the H.A. Times article. Guess we now know exactly what our mystery caller was predicting. I didn't think it would be something on this scale. Shocking."

Salome pulled her car off the road and idly watched two Amish buggies clopping through a field. "I'm on the way to Pittsburgh right now for a wedding. This was the absolute worst time for him to pull the trigger.”

“I was just about run to FedEx to drop off the packet of questions to Hank. Should I hold off?”

“No, send it. We can always send another one. In the meantime, let’s leave off investigating this new mess, because Harmon may want to handle it as a corporate espionage case rather than lay criminal charges. He would have a lot more leverage and control that way.”

“What if either one of them asks for our help?” Stewart queried, which he knew wouldn’t happen with Harmon, whose outright hatred for the FBI was well known.

Salome shrugged, even though Stewart couldn’t see it. “Then we help, and make it our investigation. Until then, let’s stay out of it. I do think that Hank’s going to go after this anonymous person who accused him, and we can probably expect a media statement that will get him summoned again.”

“Should I call him and warn him off?”

“Normally I would say no, but it might calm him to know that we’re not adding it to our pile.”

“Okay, thanks. Safe travels.”

Stewart picked up the phone and dialed Hank’s cell.

Seditionist HQ

"Fuck," mumbled Hank as his phone rang again. "Yes, Stewart? How are you on this beautiful, pleasant day, in which my world is absolutely *not* imploding around me?"

Stewart was not amused. "This is a courtesy call, Hank. I heard the news, but obviously the FBI has no jurisdiction over corporate espionage cases. We're going to stay out of it unless Harmon wants to press criminal charges, which he won't."

"Ah." That did calm Hank considerably, but... "What if he decides to?"

"He won't unless he has absolute irrefutable proof. Otherwise he will lose and have to pay the legal expenses for both of you, and his reputation would be damaged. There's nothing to gain by it. I would suggest not contacting him at this time and letting him sort it out on his end."

"Oh. Well...I, okay."

Stewart sighed. "You already talked to him, didn't you?"

"No. I just left him a message to call me. He hasn't yet."

"Okay. Like I said, no jurisdiction here, but you know I was a corporate lawyer in my past life. Don't talk to him, and don't threaten him. Everything you say or do at this point matters. Okay?"

Hank closed his eyes and took a deep breath. "Hasn't it always mattered? I can't take a shit without being criticized by the Urbanes."

Another sigh from Stewart. "You threatened him already, didn't you." It wasn't a question.

"Uh. Yeah, actually." Hank rubbed a knot on the back of his neck. "Basically said I was going to sue him for slander if he didn't name the person who talked to Hailey."

"Okay, Hank. That's...wow."

"I know. Listen, thanks for your advice. I've got to get back to writing this media statement and then get to the hospital to see my kid. Did you send the FedEx?"

"On my way now. It will arrive before 8:30am on Monday."

"Great. Can't wait. Have a good weekend."

Just as Hank said that, the call came in from Harmon. Hank picked it up immediately without a glance at Dav or Rupe.

"Harmon, I'm so sorry for that message. I'm a dick."

"Yes, you are."

"I shouldn't have threatened you."

"No, you shouldn't have. If anyone can tell you who this inside source was, it's Hailey. I have no idea, but I can assure you that I'll be sending a strongly worded memo to my entire organization letting them know that speaking to the press is always unauthorized.”

Hank swallowed hard. “Thanks. I want to repeat, I have absolutely nothing to do with this.”

“Someone in your organization does.”

“And yours. Who do you think gathered this information in the first place?”

“One of your double agents, obviously,” Harmon sputtered accusingly.

“Or an Urbane who has gone rogue and has nothing to do with me,” Hank retorted.

There was a long silence on the other line. “I probably shouldn’t tell you this now, because it might cause me to lose some early leverage. But we’ve just traced the listserv posting back to a computer in Santa Monica. So it was one of yours. I’ll delete that voicemail, Hank, and we’ll pretend it never happened. In the meantime, I want you to recall all of your double agents. If you don’t, we’re going to be having a very difficult conversation regarding what my next step is going to be. Let me know your answer by end of day tomorrow. Goodbye.”

Hank looked at Dav, who was alarmed at the blood that suddenly drained from his boss’s face.

“What did he say?” Dav asked urgently.

"Umm..." Hank was feeling dizzy again. "He...he said he'll start investigating, and we'll talk again at end of day tomorrow. Let's get that media statement done so I can get to Floyd."

CHAPTER FIVE

Harmon was smarter than most, but his biggest flaw as a strategist was that he lacked a vivid imagination. He certainly knew that there was far more to this story than just a rogue Urbane or Seditionist. Had he been able to think about it long enough, or creatively enough, his very first suspicion would have been that Yannick was somehow involved. And by extension, so was Colbert, the man who hated Hank Bancroft ten times more than anyone else.

But Harmon had no such imagination, so he asked Colbert to lead the investigation into how the information got into the wrong hands.

Seditionists HQ - Los Angeles

"Dav, I need to go to the hospital to see Floyd before he disowns me." Hank was looking at his phone; there were four missed calls from Avery and two from Floyd. "I need your suggestion on who we can trust in accounting to get involved in this mess with the receipts. I know you polygraphed everyone-"

"And everyone passed, which means we can't trust anyone," Rupert put in.

"Maybe we were asking the wrong questions," Daven answered plainly.

"Oh sure, let's just come right out with it. 'Hey, yes or no question, are you trying to get Hank Bancroft thrown in jail?' Jesus, Dav, really?"

Hank massaged his forehead with the palms of his hands. "Calm down. Before today, how many people had authorization to send anonymous payments? An exact number."

Daven looked depressed as he answered. "22."

"Alright. We can't undo that stellar decision to let everyone and their mothers have access, so let's move on. One of them has been on maternity leave, so that's 21. And now we only have one person who can do it, right?"

"Yes," Daven replied. "Yannick."

"Why him, exactly?"

"He's been around a long time. Impeccable record. Very private, and almost painfully respectful to everyone on the team."

Rupe put in unhelpfully, "Weird voice, too, but that's another story."

Hank stared at him. "Wait...what do you mean, *weird voice?*"

Rupert chuckled. "Kind of a pompous inflection, sounds likes he's talking through ten layers of cheesecloth. Annoying as fuck to listen to. Have you never met him?"

"Apparently not. I'd remember that. Okay, let's polygraph him again and offer him a 3% raise to confidentially help us with this investigation and keep an eye on things from here on out. Thanks, guys. I got to go see my kid."

Hank Bancroft had a vivid imagination, but even that wasn't enough to imagine that Yannick was a candidate for his mystery man. After all, he didn't know anything about him - about anyone in accounting, actually - and trusted Daven completely to put him in a position of such responsibility. As Vance was driving him to the hospital, he received a call from Harmon's cell phone.

"Long time, no talk. We're starting an investigation as of right now. I need more time."

Harmon sounded unconvinced. "Time for what? To come up with some kind of scheme to point the blame back at me?"

"No. Don't forget this is *your* problem, too. You need to move fast to find the person on your side who leaked this information in the first place."

"I'd love to, and you know how I can do that? By you telling me who you're paying in my office to get it! Or I could just have the FBI pull all of your financial records and comb through them over the next few months to find the mole. Everything can be traced, Hank. It's just a matter of time."

Hank was feeling incredibly smug at the moment, because he actually didn't pay his double agents at all until they decided "cash out" and quit their undercover jobs to rejoin Hank's organization. Only then would they get compensation in proportion to their accomplishments. Very few had actually taken that deal that so far, to Hank's surprise. Some agents had been with him for 7 or 8 years.

"Ignore your problem, then," Hank said flippantly. "Be prepared for more leaks, though. By the way, how do I know *you* aren't the one behind all of this?"

Harmon laughed. "Oh, I see. Trying to turn the tables on me, are you? You can't seriously think I released all my personal information. Social security number, bank accounts, everything, just to spite you."

That was exact the opening Hank was looking for, and if he didn't take it now, he might never have the chance again.

"Oh, come on. You have plenty of reasons to spite me, but you know has even more? Colbert."

"Colbert?"

"Correct. I know you chose him to lead this investigation, which is basically like sending in the wolf to count the sheep. I guarantee you he's behind this. Perhaps without your knowledge, even? You might want to check the bank account numbers that were allegedly leaked. Bet they aren't even his."

"Recall your agents, Hank," Harmon ordered tersely, now even more done with this conversation. "Then we'll talk again."

"Nope. This is where the tables are turning now: take Colbert off the investigation. Then, *after* you nail down the guilty parties and exonerate me, I'll remove agents from your organization and destroy all the information we've gathered that we could use against you if we were so inclined. You have my word. In the meantime, I'm going to continue my investigation with the assumption that I'll have as much time to conduct mine as you have to conduct yours. Are we agreed?"

"So you're basically threatening me into giving you more time?" Harmon asked in disgust.

"Threaten? No, no, don't be silly. Not at all. Technically, I think it's called blackmail," Hank said lightly, with a sarcastic laugh.

Harmon smiled - he had him now. "Right. Understood. Take all the time you need, Hank."

"Thanks! Chat with you soon, pal."

Hank disconnected the call and chuckled to himself in satisfaction.

Urbane HQ - Denver

Harmon slowly hung up the phone and turned to look at Colbert, who had blanched at least twice during the last part of call. He reached over and hit the STOP button on the tape recorder.

"You're sure that was being recorded, right?" asked Harmon skeptically.

"Yes, boss. Every word."

"And you heard him say *prepare for more leaks* and then outright blackmail me, right? I wasn't imagining it?"

"I did. Loud and clear. He was obviously joking, but..."

"Doesn't matter. We finally caught him in the act, the smug fucker. Let's make a few duplicates, then send the original to Stewart. I'm going to press criminal charges."

Colbert blanched again, panicking about having been called out and accused by Hank. "Wait. What if you...I have a better idea. What if you let Hank know we recorded that, and threaten to release it to Stewart if he doesn't cooperate?"

Harmon frowned. "Blackmail, with a blackmail attempt? That is some serpentine shit, right there. Damn."

"Or, we should wait until we have absolute proof that the listserv posting came from one of his guys. Why rush into this? It's got to be foolproof or we'll have to pay his legal bills. He hasn't yet admitted to this leak. Just threatening other leaks. I think we can nail him better than this."

Colbert was all but hyperventilating now. He could *not* let that recording get out, because Hank was right - the bank account numbers weren't his. He had transposed some numbers to protect his funds; a terrible decision, in hindsight. *Stepped on his own dick*, as Hank Bancroft would say.

Harmon was thinking as he tapped his pen against his temple. "This is all kinds of fucked up. I don't even know where to start. Do you think there's any possibility that Yannick is involved? I mean, we paid him through the nose for his past services. I can't imagine him turning against us. But he still works for them, right?"

"He had given his notice last time we spoke, a couple months ago."

"Shit. Well...maybe you're right. Let's take a few more days to get all our ducks in a row." Harmon popped the tape out of the recorder and put it carefully in his safe, while Colbert watched in silent horror.

"And of course we have to investigate our own team, too. I'm making a list of who to question first in regards to collecting all that data."

"I have an idea," Harmon said suddenly. "Let's give Yannick a call. Just ask him if he knows anyone in Hank's office who might have released our info either for him, or for his own reasons. Don't offer a penny for any kind of service. We'll start with him, and move on from there."

Colbert forced down the lump in his throat, but it took a few swallows. "Good idea. I'll call him."

Los Angeles

"Hey Dav, me again. I have to talk quick, just pulling up to the hospital. I've changed my mind. I want our entire senior accounting team placed on paid leave until further notice. All 21 of them, including Yannick. Confiscate their phones and badges, too. Laptops. Everything. We're not taking any more chances."

"I think that's-"

"Don't argue with me," Hank interrupted bitterly.

"-a wise move, I was about to say."

"Oh. Sorry. I want all of them intercepted as they arrive to work Monday morning and gathered into a conference room. Then we explain, and send them all home at once. Don't let anyone get wind of this before 8am Monday, or it could tip somebody off."

"Will do. I hope Floyd feels better soon. Say hello for me."

"I will. Thanks, Dav. By the way, I think we're going to be okay with Harmon. I sort of forced him into his own internal investigation, and now we'll have enough time to do our own."

"Forced? How?"

Hank still felt smug, and he replied lightly, "Oh, just doing what I do. Charm and wit gets you everywhere in this world."

"Okay. Well, good luck with that. Let me know when you are available to talk again."

"Will do."

CHAPTER SIX

Palisades Hospital

Los Angeles

Hank was feeling newly invigorated as Vance silently dropped him and Martinez off at the front entrance of the hospital. Press cars were already there, having tailed Avery and Brittany there hours earlier, and he could feel rather than hear the dozens of shutter clicks go off. It occurred to him too late that he should probably stop smiling, seeing as to what this errand entailed.

Floyd was asleep, so Brittany and Avery were standing at the doorway talking to each other in hushed tones as Hank walked up with Floyd's doctor on his tail.

"Room's not big enough for all of us," Hank murmured. "Why don't you guys go take a break? Is the cafeteria still open for lunch, Dr. Harborough?"

The blonde woman nodded cheerfully. "Yes indeed, 24 hours a day. But I'd stay away from the meatloaf if I were you."

The two guards left, and Hank went to sit down next to Floyd.

"Is this pretty much the same as last time?"

Dr. Harborough referred to the clipboard that was nestled in her left arm.

"Same cause, but not as drastic. I think he can go home in about 3 hours. We've given him a bag of fluid and medications for his stomach. Blood tests are all normal, at least the ones we don't have to wait a few days to hear back on. I would strongly suggest, though…"

Hank didn't want to hear about strengthening the anti-anxiety medication, and the doctor already knew he was deeply opposed to drugging his children into better moods.

"No," he said preemptively, loud enough that Floyd woke up with a start.

"Dad?"

"Sorry, kiddo. Didn't mean to wake you."

Floyd shifted around on his right side to look at his dad. "What time is it? What's going on? Why did you leave with Uncle Dav?"

Hank cleared his throat. "It's almost 2. Can't answer your other questions. I'm sorry."

"Are you in trouble again?"

"Floyd."

Hank looked up to find Theo glaring at him from his chair on the other side of Floyd's bed, but Hank ignored it. He was fully aware of what was on the boy's mind and had no interest in discussing it right now. Or ever.

"Want to go home," Floyd mumbled sleepily.

Hank looked at Dr. Harborough, who spoke up at last. "Floyd, you can go home at 5. I want you to eat something so we can make sure you're keeping food down. I'll be right back, Mr. Bancroft."

"Thanks." He waited until the door closed again before addressing his youngest. "Have you eaten?"

"Yeah. Hours ago."

"Good."

Theo's eyes narrowed. "*Hours*. Ago."

Oh boy. *That* tone. This was going to be bad.

"Right. I heard you."

"*Hours* ...in which you *weren't here* because your stupid fucking job is more important than your kids!"

Hank saw Martinez stiffen from across the room, so he stifled a rebuke and kept his tone pleasant. "Floyd, I'll be back in a minute. Theo, come with me, please."

"No."

Hank stood and latched a strong hand onto Theo's arm, effortlessly pulling him into the large bathroom that was attached to the hospital room. He didn't let go once they were in there alone.

"Theo. I hear you. I get it. But calm down or we'll be having a chat when we get home. Do you understand me?"

Theo angrily tried to wrench his arm away, in vain. "You're going to have to punish Avery then, too, because he said the same thing. You suck, dad."

Hank swallowed down the hard lump in his throat.

"Thought I told you not to be a tattletale."

"Whatever. Let me go!" This time Theo succeeded in flinging his arm loose, but there was nowhere to go; his dad was blocking the door.

"Okay. You've earned yourself a chat. But I'll make a deal with you. If you can behave yourself until we get home, I'll cancel it."

"And if I don't?" Theo challenged boldly.

"Going to be a hell of a discussion, then. Better clear your calendar for the evening." Hank stood up and calmly stepped aside to open the bathroom door for his son. "After you."

Theo hesitated, then darted through the door.

"Martinez," Hank said quietly. "You can station outside the door, if you prefer. Whatever you feel more comfortable with. I'll leave it up to you."

Just as he said that, a visibly stressed Vance showed up and quietly slipped into the room. "Boss, you got a sec?"

"What's up?"

Vance shook his head slightly and turned away, so Hank followed him into the hallway and shut the door.

"Yes?"

"There's a big crowd going nuts outside. All but calling for your blood. Took me forever to get the car parked because they were blocking the ramp to the garage."

"A big *crowd?* There were maybe a dozen people out there when we arrived."

"Not anymore, sir. Lots of people now."

"Fuck. Okay, come with me to the cafeteria to find Avery. Deveraux, stay here."

—-

As Hank strolled through the double doors, he was struck dumb by the sight that greeted him. Every single person in the cafeteria had their back to them because they stood crowded around one single television on the wall, transfixed by live imagery of the angry scene outside. Everyone, including all the cafeteria staff and his own guards.

Hank slowly walked up behind Avery, who didn't see him, while reluctantly turning his own gaze to the screen. The sound was off, but the captions told the tale loud and clear.

-STUNNING LEAK WAS ATTRI-

-BUTED TO HANK BANCROFT-

-THE SAME MAN WHO-

-APPARENTLY HAS NO QUALMS-

-SENDING HIS YOUNG SON-

-TO THE HOSPITAL ALONE-

-LEAVING HIM TO FEND FOR-

-HIMSELF FOR OVER SIX-

-HOURS. HE ARRIVED ONLY-

Goddamn .

"Avery," Hank said sharply, startling his once-favorite guard. "What are you doing?"

Avery may have been startled, but there was no worry in his expression. He was not prohibited from watching the news like Floyd was, for one thing. And he was on break, for another.

"Monitoring the latest happenings, boss. For your security, of course."

"Of course. But I need to talk to you. In private."

————-

Rupert's House

"Can't say I blame 'em, Dav. He should have been at the hospital." Rupert muted the television. "But at least we got the media statement done. Not that anyone's going to buy it. Jesus, what a cluster."

"Hmm. Do you think he's ever going to tell us who the four embedded agents are?"

"Not until he's on his deathbed."

Daven shifted uncomfortably. "You know...he won't let me tell him why I held back those receipts for so long. Didn't want to hear it."

Rupert shrugged. "Probably for the best, and you know why. He can't lie. You tell him, he tells the FBI, you get in trouble. He's protecting you."

"No, it's not that. It was something else. He *can* lie, by the way. Found that out myself last night."

"What do you mean?"

"Well..." Daven regretted having brought it up, but he did, so he had to finish the story. "He told me he had a rough flight home and it made him worry about what would happen to his kids if the plane crashed."

Rupert cocked his head. "You'd be their legal guardian. They'd go to you. He *knows* that."

"I know. That's what puzzled me, but it's not the only thing. The flight was perfectly smooth. Avery told me. Why would he lie about something like that?"

"I have no idea. That's odd. Maybe it's nothing. This whole thing is making him paranoid, and rightly so. You couldn't pay me enough to be in his shoes right now."

Daven opened his briefcase and rummaged through for a long moment before locating his target, a thickly bound version of the new indentured servant laws that had passed on March 1.

"I think the answer is in here. Between the three of us, he's the only one who's read the entire thing. Now, these statutes go into effect on April 1, right?"

"Yes. And?"

Daven sucked in a deep breath. "I was browsing this and happened to come across a clause that says *non-related legal guardians of minors are subject to the court's approval upon sentencing.*" Pause. "You know what...never mind. I've said too much already."

Rupe stared at his friend. "And not enough. What's on your mind? Just spill it, for god's sake."

"I think..." Daven bit his lower lip as he debated whether or not to say the horrible words. "I think Hank isn't worried about dying at all. Maybe he believes he's going to jail, and that the court won't approve me to take care of Theo and Floyd."

"What? He's innocent."

"That's what we think. The FBI might come to a different conclusion."

"*Daven.*" Rupert stood up as if to end the discussion. "We're not going there again. He didn't do it, end of story."

"You're not understanding what I'm saying," Daven sighed in frustration. "Our opinion doesn't matter in court. Facts do. If he's not brought down by those receipts, or those leaks, he's going to be brought down by something else. Whoever is doing this won't stop now. It's only a matter of time before the next thing happens, and we both know Hank's his own worst enemy when he's backed into a corner."

"Okay, Sherlock. I get it," Rupert snapped defensively. "So what do you propose we do, then?"

"Not us. It's really up to Hank. If he's convinced Colbert is behind this, he needs to let Harmon know and request his cooperation. In order to do that, he'll need to apologize and make peace with him first."

Rupe snorted. "Oh. Right. Good luck talking him into that one."

"If he disagrees and refuses, I'll let him know what the next step has to be if I'm right, and this keeps up. He'll want to protect the boys before anything else. If he refuses…"

"Which he *will* …then what's his plan B?"

Daven swallowed hard, then looked his friend in the eyes without flinching. "Quitting his job."

———

Palisades Hospital

Hank Bancroft was in a horrific mood after having it out with Avery about his remarks, and then learning he had to fire Lucas when he got home for making the unforgivable decision not to call him when Floyd was obviously in need of medical assistance. Theo picked up on the subtle danger instantly and dared say nothing as his dad returned and sat back down with a sigh.

"Hey, kiddo," he said to Floyd. "Dr. Harborough says you're good to go. Just waiting for the discharge paperwork."

"It's only 3."

Hank stroked Floyd's hair back into place. "Well, you're doing good enough to bail early. Listen, when we leave the hospital I want you to lay down on the back seat and relax. Close your eyes and just breathe. We'll take it really easy the rest of the weekend."

He felt Theo's eyes boring into him. The kid had seen the mob outside the window and wasn't fooled by his dad's attempt to keep Floyd from seeing them. But he also knew it was best for his brother, so he said nothing.

"How do you feel?" Hank asked.

"Headache. Tired."

"Me, too."

Theo snorted derisively at that, and his dad threw him a dirty look. "Just so you know? You got Avery in deep shit. I told you not to tattle."

The boy paled instantly. "What did you do?"

Hank ignored him. "Floyd, we have to make a decision regarding your anti-anxiety medication. I know it gives you some bad side effects, but if it's increased, these panic attacks won't be so bad. How do you feel about that?"

"Increase it," Floyd murmured. "I can't do this anymore."

"Okay." This was the first time Hank had let Floyd have any say in his medical treatment, and it was tough to let go of that control. He instantly regretted asking, because the answer was completely unexpected. Floyd hated his pills.

"Or," interjected Theo bitterly from the other side of the bed, "you can just have a boring job like normal people so that everyone's not stalking us all the time, and then Floyd wouldn't have to worry and be all drugged up just to function every day."

The truth was brutal, and it hit him like a cartoon anvil falling from the sky. That was the exact moment Hank Bancroft gave up the battle with his youngest and decided to wear his heart on his sleeve for the first time in his entire life. He looked around the room; they were alone. His throat was tight.

"Theo, you're right. We can't do this anymore. Wish granted. I've just decided I'm not going to run again in November."

Theo could only let out a tiny squeak in his surprise. His face lit up like a Christmas tree.

"You can't tell anyone," Hank continued. "I'll have to announce it in a few weeks. But tomorrow I'm going to call our builders up in Sacramento and start building the house near Yosemite. Do you understand what this means for all of us?"

"Yes. No. I don't...oh my god." He was grinning from ear to ear, and Hank said nothing more as he gave him a few minutes to process the news.

"Theo," he said eventually. Gently. "I want to talk to Floyd alone for a minute, okay? Can you do me a favor and go in the bathroom, and close the door? I'll come get you shortly."

Theo got up as if he was in a trance and did exactly as he was told. A very confused Floyd turned towards his dad.

"Dad? Why did you tell him like *that*?"

Hank shrugged and smiled a little. "Does it hurt to make him think I'm doing it for him?"

The teenager grinned sleepily. "Not if you keep letting me think you're doing it for me."

"I *am* doing it for you, Floyd."

Floyd sighed happily and closed his eyes. Hank should have been happy at this moment, too. Both his sons were on his side again, content and optimistic, and mostly behaving themselves lately. Life was good.

But all he could think about was that clause in the new laws. The one that had been running through his mind for two days like credits at the end of a movie. His heart skipped another beat as it started up all over again as he thought about how he had just stupidly and blatantly blackmailed Harmon: ... *non-related legal guardians of minors are subject to the court's approval upon sentencing of the felonious parent...*

CHAPTER SEVEN

Los Angeles - later Saturday afternoon

"Dad?" Floyd called as he made himself comfortable on his makeshift bed in the backseat. "Can we stop at Shake Shack?"

"No. Vance, straight home please. Floyd, lie down."

"I am. Can we go sailing tomorrow?"

"No. Hang on. Brittany, can you…"

"Got it," said Brittany as she got out of the car to clear the hospital's blocked driveway. Hank was impressed that she managed the task almost effortlessly and apparently with only a few words to the couple dozen angry people who stood with protest signs. It was too late to keep Theo from seeing them; he read the words and shifted his wide eyes to his dad, but said nothing.

"Dad?" came the voice from the backseat again.

"*What*, Floyd?"

"I'm hungry."

"I'll make you something when we get home."

The SUV pulled through the crowd slowly, and Hank looked back to make sure Floyd wasn't paying attention. He wasn't, and seemed content lying face down on top of all the blankets.

"Stay down. You don't look so good. Best to get you in bed when we-"

"No, I'm fine," Floyd protested. To Hank's horror he started to sit up at the worst possible moment, right when they were in the thick of the crowd. He quickly turned and administered an almighty smack to his son's rear end, much harder than he'd intended.

"I told you to lay down," he barked, feeling exactly like the total piece of shit father that he was lately.

"Ow!" Floyd yelped in surprise as he complied. "What the...sorry, I'm sorry."

"Oh my god, dad!" Theo objected loudly as he reached over the seat to try and comfort his brother. "You're so mean."

Hank fixed a glare at him. "Do you want to be next? Turn around and be quiet."

"But that's so fucked up, I can't believe you just did that!"

Hank abruptly hauled Theo facedown over his lap and held him down tightly.

"I told you to be quiet," he growled. "One more word and I'm spanking you all the way home, just like this. Got that?"

"Yes, sir," Theo answered tightly.

"Sit up. Put your seatbelt on."

Theo obeyed and kept his mouth tightly shut, although the ferocious glare he was giving his father nearly scorched Hank's eyebrows.

"Floyd, you okay?" Hank asked belatedly, but he didn't wait for an answer. Brittany rejoined the car as they passed through the kerfuffle, and Hank gave her a silent nod of grateful thanks.

As they got on the freeway, a van from channel 5 news abruptly pulled up alongside and stuck a camera out the window. Vance quickly changed lanes once, then twice more before losing them in the heavy traffic.

The entire car was dead silent except for Theo and Floyd's overlapping sniffles.

Rupert's House.

While conversing with Daven, Rupert saw a black SUV on the television screen out of the corner of his eye and grabbed the remote control to turn up the volume. An excitable young reporter was currently airing live in front of the hospital's driveway.

- has just left the hospital with his family, and it appears they're heading home. We've just learned from two Urbanes executives affected by the data breach that their bank

accounts have already been siphoned of several thousand dollars, and that might be the least of their worries. Their social security numbers were released along with more than enough info to allow false accounts opened in their names, identity theft, and other-

"Way to give people ideas, you dumbass."

Daven leaned back into his chair. "They'll do it anyway if they're so inclined."

-eager to hear what Mr. Bancroft has to say about this debacle. Of course, it hasn't been proven he was involved, but computer experts did trace the listserv posting back to a server in West Los Angeles. As we all know, that is where the Seditionist Headquarters is located.

"Yeah," grumbled Rupe, "because there aren't like five million other people in the same area who-"

"Shhhh!"

-and we're still not sure what to make of his lengthy meeting in Philadelphia yesterday, which happened to coincide with the president's trip to FBI headquarters. It's possible he was there to specifically meet with Mr. Bancroft, but that's just speculation and we don't know if they met or-

"*Everything* you say is speculation, dimwit!"

"Seriously, Rupe? I want to hear this, please."

- say for certain now is that the tide has turned against Mr. Bancroft as far as public opinion is concerned, his unexpected opposition to two crucial votes this month all but forgotten in light of this morning's news. Let's turn it over to Hailey Hendricks, who is currently outside of the Bancroft home waiting for the family's return. Hailey?"

"Oh, fuck," Rupe exclaimed as he snatched up his phone.

"Rupe," Hank answered tersely. "Not a good time."

"You're telling me. Hailey Hendricks is broadcasting live from your driveway right now."

"What? Shit, we're like a block away. Thanks, I'll call you back." He hung up. "Vance."

"Boss?"

"Turn around and take the back entrance to the house. Brittany?"

"Radioing them now, sir."

There was a rear underground entrance to the house on the street that ran along the back side of the property, but it wasn't finished yet and had no gate or paving. The guards would have to hurry to run back and remove the temporary barriers, and then Vance would have to drive over construction materials to get there, but it was doable.

"Dad?"

"Not now, Floyd. Vance, take it easy. Slow and steady so we don't beat the guards there."

"We're being followed, sir. Four cars, maybe five."

Fuck. "Okay. Go through the Shake Shack."

"Dad?"

"Be *quiet* Floyd, for god's sake!"

"But I'm going to throw up. Carsick from laying down."

"Okay, sit up. Theo, get him a bottle of water from the cooler. One for me too, please."

Vance deftly turned the car around in a cul de sac and headed back to Pico Boulevard. The Shake Shack was an excellent spot to dodge press cars; they usually didn't follow their prey through the drive-thru because they would get stuck behind the gates that wouldn't rise until food was paid for and taken at the window. There was nowhere for them to wait, either, so most of the time Vance was able to break free of tails with this method. This time, however, three press cars followed him right in as if they were all attached to each other's bumpers with a chain. As they pulled up to the speaker, Hank moved to the left side of the car and rolled down the window. There was a tiny camera pointing straight at him.

Welcome to Shake Shack, this is Aston, may I take your order?

"Good afternoon, Aston. Do you know who I am?"

Yes, sir! We're studying you at school this month.

Hank blushed, as he often did at unexpected reminders of his fame. Or infamy, as some would say. "Ah. Well, I need a big favor. We're going to pull up to your window now without ordering, okay?"

Yes, sir.

Vance pulled up slowly. Hank was afraid to know what Floyd must be thinking, but there was no time to worry about it right now.

"Aston, we just need to sit here for about five minutes like we're waiting for an order. Then I need you to stall the cars behind me for a few minutes, please. We're trying to lose them so I can get my son home safely and privately. He's been sick."

"Vultures," Aston replied in disgust. "Yes, sir, don't you worry. Would you like some coffee while you wait?'

"That would be wonderful. Thank you."

She smiled brilliantly, obviously starstruck beyond repair. "And can I ask *you* a favor, sir? I kind of secretly read my textbooks at work when business gets slow. You know? Between orders, nothing else to do. Happens a lot."

"That sounds very...dedicated." Hank wasn't sure where this was going.

Aston gleefully turned around and pulled out a Sharpie from somewhere, along with her history book. "Would you autograph this for me, Mr. Bancroft? Right here in chapter 22. There's where you first come in, way back when you were born."

Way back when? Ouch. "And how did I die?" he teased, flipping to the later chapters as if searching for an answer to his destiny.

Aston shrugged. "I don't know, we haven't gotten that far yet. Do you mind signing it?"

Hank froze. "Uh. Doesn't this book belong to your high school?"

"Not anymore. Going to steal it now." Aston grinned.

"I'll just pretend I didn't hear that." Hank dutifully signed the book, adding a "stay in school" note with a smiley face.

"Thank you! I'll get your coffee now."

Hank turned to Brittany after Aston walked away from the window, not knowing whether to laugh or cry. "*Way back when.* For fuck's sake. Like I was roaming around with the dinosaurs or something."

Brittany cleared her throat - which sounded suspiciously like a camouflaged laugh - and spoke quietly into her lapel mic to get an update from the house.

"Do you get asked for your autograph a lot, dad?" Theo asked in awe. He had never seen this happen before, because their guards always prevented strangers from getting that close to their dad everywhere they went.

"Not so much anymore. Mostly during the war, and right after."

"Did women ever ask you to sign their boobs?"

Hank almost choked on his water, and Vance let out a strangled bark.

"Seriously, Theo? Where on earth did you get that idea?"

"Saw it after a wrestling match. And a concert. I don't remember the other thing."

Hank was going to deny it, but there was nothing to be lost by lightening the mood in the car a little. "Okay, well...yeah, they did. Your dad was a stud once, you know." He winked at his son.

Theo was full of mischief suddenly. "I bet you did it. Didn't you?"

"Never, actually. I was married to your mom, and that's not acceptable behavior for a husband. For a good husband, anyway. Brittany, what did Avery say?"

"He said they need about three minutes. Working hard to clear a path."

"Thanks. Floyd, are you alright?"

"Yeah, I guess," came the grumbled, unhappy reply. He couldn't possibly be amused by anything at the moment.

Aston came back to the window with the coffee and waited until Brittany finally gave the go-ahead to leave. Hank handed the young woman $50 first. "This is for the replacement book. Just say you lost it and don't steal anything else, ever. Okay, we're ready to go. Thanks, Aston."

The gate instantly lifted up, and Vance pulled out as quickly as he could manage without actually leaving smoking tire tracks. Two seconds later the long flimsy arm fell back down again so fast that it crashed down on the roof with a bone-crunching THWACK! that made everyone jump.

"Son of a bitch!" Vance exclaimed under his breath as he floored it and turned right onto Olympic.

Hank held back laughter as he turned to look out the back window; Vance was as lovingly protective of the SUV as Hank was of his Thunderbird. "Yeah. She may have timed that poorly, but it did the trick. They're trapped. Okay, get us home."

"Goddamn, going to have a hell of a time buffing out that motherfu-"

"Vance!"

"Sorry, boss."

Sunday

The church that the leaders of The Seditionists attended had informally been considered off-limits for protests and media attention, and Hank was glad to see that today was not a break in tradition. There were, as usual, photographer's cars parked across the street and in the square, but that was all. It was almost too quiet.

Rupert and Daven were already there, and Hank took his usual place in between them.

"Hey guys," he whispered. "Surprised I didn't get any other calls last night from you two. Hailey must've shit a brick once she realized I slipped past her."

"Hank!" Daven admonished with a fierce and increasingly common *we're in church, you idiot* type of hand gesture.

Hank looked up in the balcony, where his grumpy sons were just sitting down. "You know, I have an idea. If you're not busy, why don't guys come to the servant's luncheon with us after this? It's rather fun. Not sure why I haven't invited you before."

Daven looked askance at him, but Rupert butted in first. "Would love to, thanks Hank. You would too, right Dav?"

"I would?"

"Great, it's settled then. I've always wanted to see what the famous Bancroft Sunday Bruncheon is all about."

"Why do you want us to come?" Daven asked suspiciously, ignoring the looks from Rupert that were clearly designed to shut him up.

Hank looked hurt. "Do I have to have a reason? Maybe I just want you there because you're my closest friends, and my kids idolize you. You should be there."

Daven was supremely discomfited by this gesture, since it fit neatly into his theory that that Hank was preparing to possibly lose his kids and wanted their godfathers to get more comfortable around the household. Just in case?

"I'm sorry Hank, I'm just confused. You're so secretive about your family one day, and the next you're inviting us to this. It just makes me wonder what's really-"

"Dav," Rupert said warningly. "This is not the time or place for that particular discussion."

Hank looked back and forth between the two of them. "What *particular discussion?*"

"Nothing, Hank," Daven whispered quickly, and quieter than before. "We're just not used to this. I mean, even after ten years I don't know how many servants you *have,* and now I'm about to have lunch with all of them. You're quite the secret keeper, you know, so this is...new. That's all."

Hank's nerves prickled. "We have 11, so now you know. *Secret keeper*? What does that mean, exactly? And why are you so offended about me asking you to a brunch with my household?"

"I'm not offended. I'm alarmed."

Hank raised his voice just over a whisper, although he felt like shouting. "Oh, really? Well forget it then, sorry I asked. You're uninvited."

"Thank you."

Rupert reached over and put a hand on Daven's knee, keeping his face carefully neutral. "*Stop it*, both of you. We are *in church*, in case you haven't noticed. You're acting like children."

Children. Hank looked up again at his boys, who were watching him curiously.

What's wrong? Theo mouthed.

Uncle Dav is being an asshole, Hank mouthed back.

"I understood that, Hank," Daven hissed.

"Good," Hank replied shortly, as he angrily flipped open his bible.

"Oh my god," muttered Rupert. "If you were my kids you'd both be over my knee by now. Shut up, the sermon's starting."

Hank ignored him, his mind already elsewhere, as usual. Theo had giggled at the *asshole* remark, but Floyd had no reaction at all except for a deeper scowl. He was still upset about getting smacked in the car yesterday, and Hank didn't blame him, and he flushed hotly again at the reminded. *What kind of father does that to a kid that just got out of the hospital? Oh that's right, my kind.*

Hank was stone-faced as he sat with Daven and Rupert in the limo a few hours later from the hotel back to the house. The bruncheon had gone well, but Hank refused to talk business until it was over. Now the boys were in the other car so that the three men could talk, and Hank was thoroughly ready to set fire to the Sunday newspaper he was currently holding.

"Okay, this is...they're talking about our double agents. How do they even know we have them? Has Harmon been talking to the press himself on this side? That's completely illegal."

It was true; in this era of government Hank, Daven, Rupert, Harmon, Colbert, and Umber were expressly prohibited by law from speaking to any political reporter off the record or even casually. Even to be seen greeting Hailey at a party could get any of them censured on the spot, for example. Not that Hank would ever give her the time of day, of course, except at press conferences. If Harmon had talked to the press, well…that was something.

Rupert looked deeply bored by the whole thing already. "Oh come on, we've been through this before. All Harmon had to do was tell someone like Zane, and *he* could run off and tell Hailey. You know that law is really just for show."

Hank looked sharply at his friend. "I wrote that law, Rupe, and it's not just for show."

"I'm sorry," Rupert said sincerely, feeling utterly foolish that he had forgotten that detail.

"Furthermore," Hank added, "this article claims the Urbanes don't employ double agents. That's another thing that should only be at Harmon's level of knowledge, and Colbert's. And Umber's, but certainly no lower."

"It does make us look really bad in comparison," Rupert conceded.

"And this bullshit right here." Hank jabbed angrily at a paragraph in the second article on the front page.

Sources say the FBI is currently investigating Hank Bancroft for bribery. Two men who spoke under strict conditions of anonymity reached out to a reporter at this paper to claim they were personally given $3,000 by an inside agent of

Hank Bancroft in exchange for unspecified services, and that they have the receipts to prove it. Furthermore, one of these men claims he has information on the December murder of Colbert's driver that could lead to a revelation of Mr. Bancroft's involvement in the assassination, including several calls he allegedly made to the killer just five days before the incident. As if that's not enough, at least one man who claims to work for the Seditionists in Los Angeles has let us know he offered his services to the FBI as an informant. We will be updating this column daily as this extraordinary story evolves.

There was an ugly silence in the car for a long time, which Hank eventually broke.

"Guys. What the fuck is going on?"

"We don't know," Rupert said. "We're doing everything we can, you know that. But I have a plan."

"What?" Hank rasped. "Speaking of plans, theirs is already working. I truly feel like I'm the one going crazy, not everyone else."

"Well you're not, so let's talk about it. You're convinced Colbert is behind all of this, right?"

Hank nodded. He felt like he was having an out of body experience all of a sudden.

Rupert pressed on calmly. "Right. So...you should tell Harmon that and ask for his help."

"I already did."

Daven was startled. "Oh...you did? When?"

"Friday night. He just laughed. Colbert's leading the investigation for him. I also told Stewart. Without evidence, he's completely unwilling to pursue it. So, forget that. I'm sorry I didn't tell you sooner, but it just was something I don't really want to talk about."

"That was an important thing to leave out, Hank. You have to keep us informed of these things."

Rupert nodded. "Agreed. So much for plan A."

"Yep. What's our plan B?"

Daven and Rupert looked at each other, each unwilling to tell Hank to quit his job yet. It was too soon, and there was still a lot of work to do.

"We're working on it," they said together.

CHAPTER EIGHT

Late Sunday night, Bancroft House

Four hours into his research Hank had made no discoveries, and no decisions. He hadn't picked up his phone, either, despite both Daven and Rupert trying to reach him in the past half hour. To say his despair was at its lowest ebb wouldn't have been much of an exaggeration; the worst was when Mary died. This was only a very distant second.

He threw aside the newspaper as the expected knock broke into his thoughts. "Come in."

Floyd came in reluctantly, looking for all the world like he would rather be walking over lava than get any closer to his dad.

"Sit down."

Floyd obeyed, then looked at his hands and said nothing, so Hank began without any preamble.

"You're still mad at me for what happened in the car yesterday."

Nod.

"Floyd, you *know* that when I tell you to do something, you do it, even if you don't know why. I want you to take a look at this and tell me if you can figure my reasoning for making you lie down." He picked the newspaper back up and handed it to his son. "Look at the picture. What do you see?"

"Protesters." He peered closer. "Wait, that's Brittany, and…that's our car."

"Yes, this is us as we left the hospital yesterday. Those protesters were angry with me."

Floyd picked up on his meaning immediately. "Oh. You didn't want me to see them so that I wouldn't panic again."

"Correct. Now do you see why I did what I did?"

"Yeah."

"Sorry, what was that?"

"Yes, sir," Floyd amended. His eyes darted back to a pair of familiar, unpleasant objects on the credenza. Hank followed his gaze and then felt his heart fall a little.

"I'm not going to paddle you, Floyd. You just got out of the hospital, for god's sake."

"That didn't stop you from…"

Floyd quickly trailed off and fell silent.

"Good choice not to finish that sentence, kiddo," Hank replied stiffly.

Floyd took a deep breath. "Sorry. Did you really fire Lucas, dad?"

The unexpected change of subject left Hank felt slightly disoriented for a moment. "Uh. Yes, I did. A few hours ago."

"Because of me?" Floyd wiped a stray tear from his eye. "I talked him into not calling you. Begged him. This is my fault."

"Not completely, but you did play a big part in it. Floyd, you're 16 now. Old enough to where your decisions don't affect just you alone anymore. Almost everything you do and say impacts someone else, too."

Floyd swallowed hard. This discussion was far worse than any corporal punishment.

"I'm sorry," he whispered miserably. "Please hire him back."

Hank's eyebrows raised way up. "What? You don't even like him."

"That doesn't mean I wanted this, dad."

"I'm sure he didn't, either. I just hope you'll both learn something from this and not repeat your mistakes. And I also expect you to stop sulking around, pronto. Go to bed."

"Dad."

"What?"

Floyd took a deep breath and braced himself for backlash. "You're right, I'm 16 now. Old enough to hear the truth. You could have just told me in the car you didn't want me to look out the windows because you thought it would panic me.

Maybe next time you can just tell me what's going on so that you don't even *have to* tell me what to do, and I'll just figure it out for myself."

Hank swallowed hard. Floyd was growing up so fast; it was both fascinating and difficult to witness.

"I hear you, Floyd. I do. But sometimes I don't have time to explain myself, nor should I have to even if I do. You know better. Next time, the belt comes out."

Floyd looked about to cry at that.

Hank felt hellishly sleepy all of a sudden, and his son turned to a blur for a few moments. "Okay, discussion over and you're forgiven. Just remember I'm going to protect you as long as I can now, because I'm not going to be around forever."

"Dad! Don't say that."

Hank sat back in his chair. "Sorry, I'm confused. I thought you said you were old enough to hear the truth."

"But not *that!* "

Hank didn't really have time for this, he realized. Daven and Rupert had called again, there was still the email to Stewart to finish, and he had to plan out his meetings for Monday. Nothing had been finished, only partially started and abandoned. It was already nine o'clock.

"You can't have it both ways, Floyd. Either you get treated like an adult, or like a child. Which is it? Let me know so that we can stop arguing already."

Floyd was breathing hard again. Too hard. *Fuck.* Hank stood up.

"Never mind. We're both tired, and I can see you're starting to get too stressed. Go to bed."

The intercom button light up, and Hank kept an eye on Floyd as he triggered the microphone.

"Yes?"

"Mr. Johanson's driver is at the front gate, sir. Asking if he can come in."

"Is Daven with him?"

"Yes, sir," replied Martinez.

"Tell me that, then. Let them in." He fought back his irritation (which was over nothing, admittedly) and turned to his son again. "Come on, upstairs we go."

"I know the way, dad," Floyd protested as Hank followed him out and up the stairs.

"Just checking to make sure you're going to be okay. You're red."

"I'm *fine.*"

"Okay. Goodnight." Hank turned and went back down the stairs to the front door, where Daven had just exited his car.

"I need some air. Let's walk."

Daven stared at him. "What's wrong?"

"Nothing. Haven't really taken advantage of all these grounds. With these walls, we could plan World War 3 and no one would ever know. Why are you here, Dav? It's kind of late. Not that I mind, but you've got me worried."

"Right. Well, first of all, because you didn't pick up your phone. Secondly, because Rupert and I feel like it would be best if you took a couple of days off and just let us work on this thing while you stay out of the spotlight."

"Yeah. Sounds good."

Daven stared again. "Really? We were sure you'd fight me about this."

"I'm guessing you drew the short straw when you guys were deciding who had to come over and give me this suggestion."

"No. Rock, paper, scissors. Something I learned from Floyd and Theo."

"Always go rock."

"I went paper."

"That's what you get. Anyway, I'm not mad. I can work from home and do a few things without causing chaos at the office."

Hank cleared his throat and tried to ignore his racing heart. "I, uh...you know what, Dav. There's something I need to ask you. You're not going to like it."

"Yes?"

Hank hesitated and didn't say anything for a while. Daven didn't prompt him.

"Okay," he said eventually. "I've asked you before, but you didn't seem sure about your answer. Do you *really* want to be the legal guardian to my sons? And don't get mad, but it's just...at the banquet, you seemed so uncomfortable and unhappy. Awkward as hell. I felt like you didn't want to get to know the household at all, or maybe you and the boys just aren't as close as I thought you were. And it's okay if so, it really is. They're a huge, life-changing responsibility."

Daven looked crushed. "I'm sorry, Hank. I just...I don't think I'm ready to be a father to them. And it's not because of them. It's because of you."

"What?" Hank askance, looking confused. "What does that even mean?"

"You're acting like they're going to be handed over to me tomorrow. I can't accept that you won't be around for longer than that. Why don't you just tell me what's going on and stop dropping hints all over the place?"

"I'm not dropping hints! I'm being realistic. Dav, I could be killed in a car accident in the morning. Or a week from now. I guess I just started worrying once I realized how short life is in the past few months."

Daven said plainly. "You're lying. You also lied about having a rough flight home on Friday, you lied about why you wanted me and Rupe at the banquet, and you've been lying by omission for weeks in regards to what's going on between you and Harmon. Tell me the truth now, or I'm going to walk away and not come back for any reason. I'm dead serious, Hank."

Hank had stopped in his tracks some time ago, and he found himself unable to move or speak for several long moments.

"This is the only chance I'm giving you," Daven continued. "Because we both know tomorrow is going to be too late."

Hank stuffed his hands inside his coat; he was freezing now, but it wasn't the temperature. "Fine. Ten years ago I visited Colbert in prison to apologize to him for what I'd done to bring him down, because for some absurd reason I felt guilty about it. You know what he said to me?"

"What?"

"He thanked me for visiting him, and then said he would return the favor someday."

Daven was unimpressed. "Okay. That's nothing. People make threats all the time, Hank."

"It was more than a threat. It was a promise. I can still see his face, and hear his tone, and feel my body go numb every time I think of it. He's been obsessed with me ever since. Even Harmon mentions it on occasion. This whole thing has been years in the making, Dav."

"Then we have years of trails to follow."

"No. He learned his lesson the first time about not leaving trails. How do you think I got him?"

They walked in silence for a few more minutes until Hank had the courage to speak again.

"It's not that I'm giving up or anything. I want to fight this." He thought about how he had blackmailed Harmon, but decided not to mention it at the moment. "But the truth is, Dav...I always knew this was coming. That it was only a matter of time."

"That has to be difficult to live with."

"Yeah. Going back to Harmon. I've been going after him so hard over the years for several reasons, all of which you know...but also because I knew that if he goes down, so does Colbert."

Daven paled a little. "Oh. That explains a lot."

"Then I started to become friendly with him, of all things...and *that's* when Colbert swooped in and got me. I let my guard down, Dav. Turns out I actually like Harmon, who'd have thought? What a cluster fuck."

"Likeable or not, he got Janet killed. You know that. God knows what else he's done."

Hank went so quiet for a minute that Daven thought he'd gotten separated from him in the dark.

"Hank?"

"Right here. We don't need God to tell us what Harmon's done, Dav. We've got double agents for that. And if I'm going down, so is he."

www.ingramcontent.com/pod-product-compliance
Lightning Source LLC
Chambersburg PA
CBHW060558100726
47907CB00005B/1430